Twist and Ernest

Ernest Series ™

Twist and Ernest is part of the Ernest Series.

Barnesyard Books and Ernest are trademarks of Barnesyard Books, Inc.

Book design by Christine Wolstenholme

Published by Barnesyard Books, Stockton, NJ 08559
www.barnesyardbooks.com

Printed in China

Library of Congress Catalog Card Number: 99-96308

ISBN 0-9674681-0-8

Twist and Ernest

by Laura T. Barnes

Illustrated by Carol A. Camburn

Stockton, NJ 08559 • www.barnesyardbooks.com

To Mrs. LaFollette's 1998-99 Colton Elementary School 4th Grade Class.
Your interest, insight and encouragement helped my dream become a reality.
May all of your own dreams also come true.

– L.T.B.

To James, and my family and friends who have supported me.

– C.A.C.

Ernest is not just any donkey. He's a scruffy, little miniature donkey. He stands just over two feet tall. Ernest has long ears that are as big as his face. He has a thick, shaggy brown coat with a furry white belly. He has little short legs, with teeny, tiny hooves.

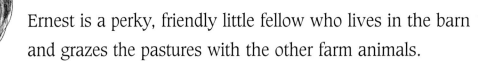

Ernest is a perky, friendly little fellow who lives in the barn and grazes the pastures with the other farm animals.

Jane, the cow, and Clarabelle, her calf, graze the pastures with Ernest. But they don't pay much attention to him.

The chickens are friendly and sometimes share Ernest's grain when he's not looking. But they don't pay much attention to the little donkey either.

Ernest was lonely. He needed a buddy. A friend to spend his days with. Someone besides the cows and the chickens.

One spring day, while Ernest was grazing, a truck with a big trailer backed up to the pasture gates.

Ernest perked his head up and looked toward the gate to see what was going on.

The door to the trailer opened and out trotted a beautiful, tall, copper horse with a big white blaze on his forehead.

Ernest stared. He couldn't believe it. It was a horse! He could be friends with a horse. The friend he was hoping for was here at last!

Ernest started to prance and buck, throwing his hind legs up with delight.

The new horse's name was Twist. He was a big, beautiful show horse. He was much, much bigger than Ernest.

Twist was used to roaming the pastures with other fancy show horses. His old friends were tall and handsome with beautiful, brushed coats and shiny manes and tails just like him.

Twist held his head and tail high and pranced his way into the pasture.

He looked at the scruffy little donkey and frowned. He didn't want to be here with him.

Twist turned away with a snort.

But there was no discouraging Ernest. He was far too excited.
He galloped and bucked and snorted with glee. "Hee haw, hee haw,
I have a new friend. Yea for me!"

He raced in circles around Twist saying, "Hello, hello. Welcome.
I am so glad you're here! I've been so lonely, and now I have a
friend to share my home with."

Twist simply looked the other way.

Ernest continued talking, "I need to tell you all about your new home. We have two cows, but they're cows. Plus, they have each other.

"We also have a bunch of noisy chickens and roosters. But they are always crowing and hanging around my grain box trying to get to my food.

"Don't worry about the cows and the chickens. You can have *me* as your friend. We are going to have so much fun together!" said Ernest.

"Oh no," thought Twist. "I am not going to be stuck with this scruffy, little donkey."

Ernest did not realize that Twist didn't want to be his friend. So Ernest went right on chatting, "Here, follow me, let me show you around."

Twist didn't want to follow the little donkey. But Twist didn't have anything better to do. So he slowly followed Ernest.

"Come on," Ernest said trotting away. He walked over to the stream. "This is our pond and stream. We can get water any time we want. I bet you're thirsty. Come on, have a sip."

Twist had to admit the long ride in the horse trailer had made him thirsty. He took a long drink of the cool water.

Twist realized that Ernest was right. It will be nice to drink from the icy stream every day. Twist just hoped the little donkey would not follow him every time he needed a drink!

"Okay, okay," continued Ernest, "my tour is not done. Just look at this beautiful green pasture. It's ours. The whole thing. We can eat and eat until our bellies are full."

Twist looked at the little donkey and thought, "What is this *'we'* stuff? Don't think I'm going to hang around with you. You're too little and I can't spend all my time with a scruffy donkey!"

Ernest was far too excited at finding a new friend to notice that Twist was not happy to have a little donkey by his side.

"Hee haw, hee haw!" said Ernest excitedly. "Now for the best part. Come on, come on," he said as he walked toward the barn. "This is our stable. We get grain and hay every night. I never miss this. It's my favorite time of day. Now we can eat together. Yea for us!"

Twist had to admit this place was nice. He was even getting used to the little donkey. Ernest was a happy fellow and he was even sort of cute. Twist was beginning to like his new home and his new friend.

Twist decided to wander around the pasture. He walked to one side of the field and then the other. It was very big and had plenty of green grass. He ate in the field for a long time. Ernest ate right beside him.

After awhile Ernest stopped munching on grass and looked at Twist. He watched as Twist stretched his neck around trying to scratch his belly. He stretched and stretched but Twist couldn't reach. He then lifted his back hoof and tried to scratch his belly with his hoof. No matter how much he tried, Twist couldn't scratch his belly.

Ernest moved closer and said, "Here let me help." He was so tiny that he could stand right under Twist. Ernest lifted his head slightly and started to scratch Twist's belly with his teeth.

"Ah, that feels good. Thank you," said Twist. "Thank you for scratching my belly. That feels much better."

"Sure," said Ernest. "What are friends for?"

Twist realized that Ernest was right. Ernest was becoming his friend.

Twist's first day turned into many peaceful days.
Gradually Twist and Ernest fell into their daily habit.
They ate in the pasture during the early morning hours
when the sun was bright, the air was cool and all was quiet.

As the morning hours ended, they would go down to the stream and take a nice
long, cool sip of water and then go up to the barn. They liked to stay in their stable
throughout the afternoon. It was cooler there. They lay down and took a long
afternoon nap together in the quiet surroundings.

Soon the two became best friends. The difference in their size did not matter.

Wherever Ernest was, Twist was right beside him.

Ernest was no longer lonely. He had finally found the friend he had been hoping for.
Twist found a peaceful and relaxing home. And, like Ernest, Twist had found
a very special friend. A friend different than he ever imagined.
But sometimes they are the best friends of all.